“Sentences to eat with a spoon, and funny like nothing else on earth”

Tilda Swinton

A
WODEHOUSE
Pick-Me-Up!

Mulliner's Buck-U-Uppo

arrow books

1 3 5 7 9 10 8 6 4 2

Arrow Books
20 Vauxhall Bridge Road
London SW1V 2SA

Arrow Books is part of the Penguin Random House group of companies
whose addresses can be found at global.penguinrandomhouse.com

Penguin Random House UK

'Mulliner's Buck-U-Uppo' from *Meet Mr Mulliner*, first published
in the United Kingdom by Herbert Jenkins Ltd in 1927
'The Spot of Art' from *Very Good, Jeeves*, first published in the
United Kingdom by Herbert Jenkins Ltd in 1930
'Strychnine in the Soup' from *Mulliner Nights*, first published in the
United Kingdom by Herbert Jenkins Ltd in 1933
All published by Arrow Books in 2008
This collection first published in the United Kingdom by Arrow Books in 2017

www.penguin.co.uk

www.wodehouse.co.uk

A CIP catalogue record for this book is available from the British Library.

ISBN 9781787460140

Typeset in 12/14 pt Perpetua Std by Jouve (UK), Milton Keynes
Printed and bound in Great Britain by Clays Ltd, St Ives Plc

MIX
Paper from
responsible sources
FSC
www.fsc.org
FSC® C018179

Penguin Random House is committed to a
sustainable future for our business, our readers
and our planet. This book is made from Forest
Stewardship Council® certified paper.

CONTENTS

MULLINER'S BUCK-U-UPPO

The village Choral Society had been giving a performance of Gilbert and Sullivan's 'Sorcerer' in aid of the Church Organ Fund; and, as we sat in the window of the Angler's Rest, smoking our pipes, the audience came streaming past us down the little street. Snatches of song floated to our ears, and Mr Mulliner began to croon in unison.

'"Ah me! I was a pa-ale you-oung curate then!"' chanted Mr Mulliner in the rather snuffling voice in which the amateur singer seems to find it necessary to render the old songs.

'Remarkable,' he said, resuming his natural tones, 'how fashions change, even in clergymen. There are very few pale young curates nowadays.'

'True,' I agreed. 'Most of them are beefy young fellows who rowed for their colleges. I don't believe I have ever seen a pale young curate.'

'You never met my nephew Augustine, I think?'

'Never.'

'The description in the song would have fitted him perfectly. You will want to hear all about my nephew Augustine.'

At the time of which I am speaking (said Mr Mulliner) my nephew Augustine was a curate, and very young and extremely pale. As a boy he had completely outgrown his strength, and I rather think that at his Theological College some of the wilder spirits must have bullied him; for when he went to Lower Briskett-in-the-Midden to assist the vicar, the Rev. Stanley Brandon, in his cure of souls, he was as meek and mild a young man as you could meet in a day's journey. He had flaxen hair, weak blue eyes, and the general demeanour of a saintly but timid cod-fish. Precisely, in short, the sort of young curate who seems to have been so common in the 'eighties, or whenever it was that Gilbert wrote 'The Sorcerer'.

The personality of his immediate superior did little or nothing to help him to overcome his native diffidence. The Rev. Stanley Brandon was a huge and sinewy man of violent temper, whose red face and glittering eyes might well have intimidated the toughest curate. The Rev. Stanley had been a heavyweight boxer at Cambridge, and I gather from Augustine that he seemed to be always on the point of introducing into debates on parish matters the methods which had made him so successful in the roped ring. I remember Augustine telling me that once, on the occasion when he had ventured to oppose the other's views in the matter of decorating the church for the

Harvest Festival, he thought for a moment that the vicar was going to drop him with a right hook to the chin. It was some quite trivial point that had come up – a question as to whether the pumpkin would look better in the apse or the clerestory, if I recollect rightly – but for several seconds it seemed as if blood was about to be shed.

Such was the Rev. Stanley Brandon. And yet it was to the daughter of this formidable man that Augustine Mulliner had permitted himself to lose his heart. Truly, Cupid makes heroes of us all.

Jane was a very nice girl, and just as fond of Augustine as he was of her. But, as each lacked the nerve to go to the girl's father and put him abreast of the position of affairs, they were forced to meet surreptitiously. This jarred upon Augustine, who, like all the Mulliners, loved the truth and hated any form of deception. And one evening, as they paced beside the laurels at the bottom of the vicarage garden, he rebelled.

'My dearest,' said Augustine, 'I can no longer brook this secrecy. I shall go into the house immediately and ask your father for your hand.'

Jane paled and clung to his arm. She knew so well that it was not her hand but her father's foot which he would receive if he carried out this mad scheme.

'No, no, Augustine! You must not!'

'But, darling, it is the only straightforward course.'

'But not to-night. I beg of you, not to-night.'

'Why not?'

'Because father is in a very bad temper. He has just

had a letter from the bishop, rebuking him for wearing too many orphreys on his chasuble, and it has upset him terribly. You see, he and the bishop were at school together, and father can never forget it. He said at dinner that if old Boko Bickerton thought he was going to order him about he would jolly well show him.'

'And the bishop comes here to-morrow for the Confirmation services!' gasped Augustine.

'Yes. And I'm so afraid they will quarrel. It's such a pity father hasn't some other bishop over him. He always remembers that he once hit this one in the eye for pouring ink on his collar, and this lowers his respect for his spiritual authority. So you won't go in and tell him to-night, will you?'

'I will not,' Augustine assured her with a slight shiver.

'And you will be sure to put your feet in hot mustard and water when you get home? The dew has made the grass so wet.'

'I will indeed, dearest.'

'You are not strong, you know.'

'No, I am not strong.'

'You ought to take some really good tonic.'

'Perhaps I ought. Good night, Jane.'

'Good night, Augustine.'

The lovers parted. Jane slipped back into the vicarage, and Augustine made his way to his cosy rooms in the High Street. And the first thing he noticed on entering was a parcel on the table, and beside it a letter.

He opened it listlessly, his thoughts far away.

'My dear Augustine.'

He turned to the last page and glanced at the signature. The letter was from his Aunt Angela, the wife of my brother, Wilfred Mulliner. You may remember that I once told you the story of how these two came together. If so, you will recall that my brother Wilfred was the eminent chemical researcher who had invented, among other specifics, such world-famous preparations as Mulliner's Raven Gipsy Face-Cream and the Mulliner Snow of the Mountains Lotion. He and Augustine had never been particularly intimate, but between Augustine and his aunt there had always existed a warm friendship.

My dear Augustine (wrote Angela Mulliner),

I have been thinking so much about you lately, and I cannot forget that, when I saw you last, you seemed very fragile and deficient in vitamins. I do hope you take care of yourself.

I have been feeling for some time that you ought to take a tonic, and by a lucky chance Wilfred has just invented one which he tells me is the finest thing he has ever done. It is called Buck-U-Uppo, and acts directly on the red corpuscles. It is not yet on the market, but I have managed to smuggle a sample bottle from Wilfred's laboratory, and I want you to try it at once. I am sure it is just what you need.

Your affectionate aunt,

Angela Mulliner.

P.S. – You take a tablespoonful before going to bed, and another just before breakfast.

Augustine was not an unduly superstitious young man, but the coincidence of this tonic arriving so soon after Jane had told him that a tonic was what he needed affected him deeply. It seemed to him that this thing must have been meant. He shook the bottle, uncorked it, and, pouring out a liberal tablespoonful, shut his eyes and swallowed it.

The medicine, he was glad to find, was not unpleasant to the taste. It had a slightly pungent flavour, rather like old boot-soles beaten up in sherry. Having taken the dose, he read for a while in a book of theological essays, and then went to bed.

And as his feet slipped between the sheets, he was annoyed to find that Mrs Wardle, his housekeeper, had once more forgotten his hot-water bottle.

'Oh, dash!' said Augustine.

He was thoroughly upset. He had told the woman over and over again that he suffered from cold feet and could not get to sleep unless the dogs were properly warmed up. He sprang out of bed and went to the head of the stairs.

'Mrs Wardle!' he cried.

There was no reply.

'Mrs Wardle!' bellowed Augustine in a voice that rattled the window-panes like a strong nor'-easter. Until to-night he had always been very much afraid of his housekeeper and had both walked and talked softly in her presence. But now he was conscious of a strange new fortitude. His head was singing a little, and he felt equal to a dozen Mrs Wardles.

Shuffling footsteps made themselves heard.

'Well, what is it now?' asked a querulous voice.

Augustine snorted.

'I'll tell you what it is now,' he roared. 'How many times have I told you always to put a hot-water bottle in my bed? You've forgotten it again, you old cloth-head!'

Mrs Wardle peered up, astounded and militant.

'Mr Mulliner, I am not accustomed—'

'Shut up!' thundered Augustine. 'What I want from you is less back-chat and more hot-water bottles. Bring it up at once, or I leave to-morrow. Let me endeavour to get it into your concrete skull that you aren't the only person letting rooms in this village. Any more lip and I walk straight round the corner, where I'll be appreciated. Hot-water bottle ho! And look slippy about it.'

'Yes, Mr Mulliner. Certainly, Mr Mulliner. In one moment, Mr Mulliner.'

'Action! Action!' boomed Augustine. 'Show some speed. Put a little snap into it.'

'Yes, yes, most decidedly, Mr Mulliner,' replied the chastened voice from below.

An hour later, as he was dropping off to sleep, a thought crept into Augustine's mind. Had he not been a little brusque with Mrs Wardle? Had there not been in his manner something a shade abrupt – almost rude? Yes, he decided regretfully, there had. He lit a candle and reached for the diary which lay on the table at his bedside.

He made an entry.

The meek shall inherit the earth. Am I sufficiently meek? I wonder. This evening, when reproaching Mrs Wardle, my worthy housekeeper, for omitting to place a hot-water bottle in my bed, I spoke quite crossly. The provocation was severe, but still I was surely to blame for allowing my passions to run riot. Mem: Must guard agst this.

But when he woke next morning, different feelings prevailed. He took his ante-breakfast dose of Buck-U-Uppo: and looking at the entry in the diary, could scarcely believe that it was he who had written it. 'Quite cross?' Of course he had been quite cross. Wouldn't anybody be quite cross who was for ever being persecuted by beetle-wits who forgot hot-water bottles?

Erasing the words with one strong dash of a thick-leaded pencil, he scribbled in the margin a hasty 'Mashed potatoes! Served the old idiot right!' and went down to breakfast.

He felt most amazingly fit. Undoubtedly, in asserting that this tonic of his acted forcefully upon the red corpuscles, his Uncle Wilfred had been right. Until that moment Augustine had never supposed that he had any red corpuscles; but now, as he sat waiting for Mrs Wardle to bring him his fried egg, he could feel them dancing about all over him. They seemed to be forming rowdy parties and sliding down his spine. His eyes sparkled, and from sheer joy of living he sang a few bars from the hymn for those of riper years at sea.

He was still singing when Mrs Wardle entered with a dish.

'What's this?' demanded Augustine, eyeing it dangerously.

'A nice fried egg, sir.'

'And what, pray, do you mean by nice? It may be an amiable egg. It may be a civil, well-meaning egg. But if you think it is fit for human consumption, adjust that impression. Go back to your kitchen, woman; select another; and remember this time that you are a cook, not an incinerating machine. Between an egg that is fried and an egg that is cremated there is a wide and substantial difference. This difference, if you wish to retain me as a lodger in these far too expensive rooms, you will endeavour to appreciate.'

The glowing sense of well-being with which Augustine had begun the day did not diminish with the passage of time. It seemed, indeed, to increase. So full of effervescing energy did the young man feel that, departing from his usual custom of spending the morning crouched over the fire, he picked up his hat, stuck it at a rakish angle on his head, and sallied out for a healthy tramp across the fields.

It was while he was returning, flushed and rosy, that he observed a sight which is rare in the country districts of England – the spectacle of a bishop running. It is not often in a place like Lower Briskett-in-the-Midden that you see a bishop at all; and when you do he is either riding in a stately car or pacing at a dignified walk. This one was sprinting like a Derby winner, and Augustine paused to drink in the sight.

The bishop was a large, burly bishop, built for endurance rather than speed; but he was making excellent going. He flashed past Augustine in a whirl of flying gaiters: and then, proving himself thereby no mere specialist but a versatile all-round athlete, suddenly dived for a tree and climbed rapidly into its branches. His motive, Augustine readily divined, was to elude a rough, hairy dog which was toiling in his wake. The dog reached the tree a moment after his quarry had climbed it, and stood there, barking.

Augustine strolled up.

'Having a little trouble with the dumb friend, bish?' he asked, genially.

The bishop peered down from his eyrie.

'Young man,' he said, 'save me!'

'Right most indubitably ho!' replied Augustine. 'Leave it to me.'

Until to-day he had always been terrified of dogs, but now he did not hesitate. Almost quicker than words can tell, he picked up a stone, discharged it at the animal, and whooped cheerily as it got home with a thud. The dog, knowing when he had had enough, removed himself at some forty-five m.p.h.; and the bishop, descending cautiously, clasped Augustine's hand in his.

'My preserver!' said the bishop.

'Don't give it another thought,' said Augustine, cheerily. 'Always glad to do a pal a good turn. We clergymen must stick together.'

'I thought he had me for a minute.'

'Quite a nasty customer. Full of rude energy.'

The bishop nodded.

'His eye was not dim, nor his natural force abated. Deuteronomy xxxiv. 7,' he agreed. 'I wonder if you can direct me to the vicarage? I fear I have come a little out of my way.'

'I'll take you there.'

'Thank you. Perhaps it would be as well if you did not come in. I have a serious matter to discuss with old Pieface – I mean, with the Rev. Stanley Brandon.'

'I have a serious matter to discuss with his daughter. I'll just hang about the garden.'

'You are a very excellent young man,' said the bishop, as they walked along. 'You are a curate, eh?'

'At present. But,' said Augustine, tapping his companion on the chest, 'just watch my smoke. That's all I ask you to do – just watch my smoke.'

'I will. You should rise to great heights – to the very top of the tree.'

'Like you did just now, eh? Ha, ha!'

'Ha, ha!' said the bishop. 'You young rogue!'

He poked Augustine in the ribs.

'Ha, ha, ha!' said Augustine.

He slapped the bishop on the back.

'But all joking aside,' said the bishop as they entered the vicarage grounds, 'I really shall keep my eye on you and see that you receive the swift preferment which your talents and character deserve. I say to you, my dear young friend, speaking seriously and weighing my words, that the way you picked that dog off with that stone was the smoothest thing I ever saw. And I am a man who always tells the strict truth.'

'Great is truth and mighty above all things. Esdras iv. 41,' said Augustine.

He turned away and strolled towards the laurel bushes, which were his customary meeting-place with Jane. The bishop went on to the front door and rang the bell.

Although they had made no definite appointment, Augustine was surprised when the minutes passed and no Jane appeared. He did not know that she had been told off by her father to entertain the bishop's wife that morning, and show her the sights of Lower Briskett-in-the-Midden. He waited some quarter of an hour with growing impatience, and was about to leave when suddenly from the house there came to his ears the sound of voices raised angrily.

He stopped. The voices appeared to proceed from a room on the ground floor facing the garden.

Running lightly over the turf, Augustine paused outside the window and listened. The window was open at the bottom, and he could hear quite distinctly.

The vicar was speaking in a voice that vibrated through the room.

'Is that so?' said the vicar.

'Yes, it is!' said the bishop.

'Ha, ha!'

'Ha, ha! to you, and see how you like it!' rejoined the bishop with spirit.

Augustine drew a step closer. It was plain that Jane's fears had been justified and that there was serious trouble afoot between these two old schoolfellows. He peeped in. The vicar, his hands behind his coat-tails, was striding up and down the carpet, while the bishop, his back to the fireplace, glared defiance at him from the hearth-rug.

'Who ever told you you were an authority on chasubles?' demanded the vicar.

'That's all right who told me,' rejoined the bishop.

'I don't believe you know what a chasuble is.'

'Is that so?'

'Well, what is it, then?'

'It's a circular cloak hanging from the shoulders, elaborately embroidered with a pattern and with orphreys. And you can argue as much as you like, young Pieface, but you can't get away from the fact that there are too many orphreys on yours. And what I'm telling you is that you've jolly well got to switch off a few of those orphreys or you'll get it in the neck.'

The vicar's eyes glittered furiously.

'Is that so?' he said. 'Well, I just won't, so there! And it's like your cheek coming here and trying to high-hat me. You seem to have forgotten that I knew you when you were an inky-faced kid at school, and that, if I liked, I could tell the world one or two things about you which would probably amuse it.'

'My past is an open book.'

'Is it?' The vicar laughed malevolently. 'Who put the white mouse in the French master's desk?'

The bishop started.

'Who put jam in the dormitory prefect's bed?' he retorted.

'Who couldn't keep his collar clean?'

'Who used to wear a dickey?' The bishop's wonderful organ-like voice, whose softest whisper could be heard throughout a vast cathedral, rang out in tones of thunder. 'Who was sick at the house supper?'

The vicar quivered from head to foot. His rubicund face turned a deeper crimson.

'You know jolly well,' he said, in shaking accents, 'that there was something wrong with the turkey. Might have upset any one.'

'The only thing wrong with the turkey was that you ate too much of it. If you had paid as much attention to developing your soul as you did to developing your tummy, you might by now,' said the bishop, 'have risen to my own eminence.'

'Oh, might I?'

'No, perhaps I am wrong. You never had the brain.'

The vicar uttered another discordant laugh.

'Brain is good! We know all about your eminence, as you call it, and how you rose to that eminence.'

'What do you mean?'

'You are a bishop. How you became one we will not inquire.'

'What do you mean?'

'What I say. We will not inquire.'

'Why don't you inquire?'

'Because,' said the vicar, 'it is better not!'

The bishop's self-control left him. His face contorted with fury, he took a step forward. And simultaneously Augustine sprang lightly into the room.

'Now, now, now!' said Augustine. 'Now, now, now, now, now!'

The two men stood transfixed. They stared at the intruder dumbly.

'Come, come!' said Augustine.

The vicar was the first to recover. He glowered at Augustine.

'What do you mean by jumping through my window?' he thundered. 'Are you a curate or a harlequin?'

Augustine met his gaze with an unfaltering eye.

'I am a curate,' he replied, with a dignity that well became him. 'And, as a curate, I cannot stand by and see two superiors of the cloth, who are moreover old schoolfellows, forgetting themselves. It isn't right. Absolutely not right, my dear old superiors of the cloth.'

The vicar bit his lip. The bishop bowed his head.

'Listen,' proceeded Augustine, placing a hand on the shoulder of each. 'I hate to see you two dear good chaps quarrelling like this.'

'He started it,' said the vicar, sullenly.

'Never mind who started it.' Augustine silenced the bishop with a curt gesture as he made to speak. 'Be sensible, my dear fellows. Respect the decencies of debate. Exercise a little good-humoured give-and-take. You say,' he went on, turning to the bishop, 'that our good friend here has too many orphreys on his chasuble?'

'I do. And I stick to it.'

'Yes, yes, yes. But what,' said Augustine, soothingly, 'are a few orphreys between friends? Reflect! You and our worthy vicar here were at school together. You are bound by the sacred ties of the old Alma Mater. With him you sported on the green. With him you shared a crib and threw inked darts in the hour supposed to be devoted to the study of French. Do these things mean nothing to you? Do these memories touch no chord?' He turned appealingly from one to the other. 'Vicar! Bish!'

The vicar had moved away and was wiping his eyes. The bishop fumbled for a pocket-handkerchief. There was a silence.

'Sorry, Pieface,' said the bishop, in a choking voice.

'Shouldn't have spoken as I did, Boko,' mumbled the vicar.

'If you want to know what I think,' said the bishop, 'you are right in attributing your indisposition at the house supper to something wrong with the turkey. I recollect saying at the time that the bird should never have been served in such a condition.'

'And when you put that white mouse in the French master's desk,' said the vicar, 'you performed one of the noblest services to humanity of which there is any record. They ought to have made you a bishop on the spot.'

'Pieface!'

'Boko!'

The two men clasped hands.

'Splendid!' said Augustine. 'Everything hotsy-totsy now?'

'Quite, quite,' said the vicar.

'As far as I am concerned, completely hotsy-totsy,' said the bishop. He turned to his old friend solicitously. 'You will continue to wear all the orphreys you want – will you not, Pieface?'

'No, no. I see now that I was wrong. From now on, Boko, I abandon orphreys altogether.'

'But, Pieface—'

'It's all right,' the vicar assured him. 'I can take them or leave them alone.'

'Splendid fellow!' The bishop coughed to hide his emotion, and there was another silence. 'I think, perhaps,' he went on, after a pause, 'I should be leaving you now, my dear chap, and going in search of my wife. She is with your daughter, I believe, somewhere in the village.'

'They are coming up the drive now.'

'Ah, yes, I see them. A charming girl, your daughter.'

Augustine clapped him on the shoulder.

'Bish,' he exclaimed, 'you said a mouthful. She is the dearest, sweetest girl in the whole world. And I should be glad, vicar, if you would give your consent to our immediate union. I love Jane with a good man's fervour, and I am happy to inform you that my sentiments are returned. Assure us, therefore, of your approval, and I will go at once and have the banns put up.'

The vicar leaped as though he had been stung. Like so many vicars, he had a poor opinion of curates, and he had always regarded Augustine as rather below than above the general norm or level of the despised class.

'What!' he cried.

'A most excellent idea,' said the bishop, beaming. 'A very happy notion, I call it.'

'My daughter!' The vicar seemed dazed. 'My daughter marry a curate!'

'You were a curate once yourself, Pieface.'

'Yes, but not a curate like that.'

'No!' said the bishop. 'You were not. Nor was I. Better for us both had we been. This young man, I would have you know, is the most outstandingly excellent young man I have ever encountered. Are you aware that scarcely an hour ago he saved me with the most consummate address from a large shaggy dog with black spots and a kink in his tail? I was sorely pressed, Pieface, when this young man came up and, with a readiness of resource and an accuracy of aim which it would be impossible to over-praise, got that dog in the short ribs with a rock and sent him flying.'

The vicar seemed to be struggling with some powerful emotion. His eyes had widened.

'A dog with black spots?'

'Very black spots. But no blacker, I fear, than the heart they hid.'

'And he really plugged him in the short ribs?'

'As far as I could see, squarely in the short ribs.'

The vicar held out his hand.

'Mulliner,' he said, 'I was not aware of this. In the light of the facts which have just been drawn to my attention, I have no hesitation in saying that my objections are removed. I have had it in for that dog since the second Sunday before Septuagesima, when he pinned me by the ankle as I paced beside the river composing a sermon on Certain Alarming Manifestations of the So-called Modern Spirit. Take Jane. I give my consent freely. And may she be as happy as any girl with such a husband ought to be.'

A few more affecting words were exchanged, and then the bishop and Augustine left the house. The bishop was silent and thoughtful.

'I owe you a great deal, Mulliner,' he said at length.

'Oh, I don't know,' said Augustine. 'Would you say that?'

'A very great deal. You saved me from a terrible disaster. Had you not leaped through that window at that precise juncture and intervened, I really believe I should have pasted my dear old friend Brandon in the eye. I was sorely exasperated.'

'Our good vicar can be trying at times,' agreed Augustine.

'My fist was already clenched, and I was just hauling

off for the swing when you checked me. What the result would have been, had you not exhibited a tact and discretion beyond your years, I do not like to think. I might have been unfrocked.' He shivered at the thought, though the weather was mild. 'I could never have shown my face at the Athenæum again. But, tut, tut!' went on the bishop, patting Augustine on the shoulder, 'let us not dwell on what might have been. Speak to me of yourself. The vicar's charming daughter – you really love her?'

'I do, indeed.'

The bishop's face had grown grave.

'Think well, Mulliner,' he said. 'Marriage is a serious affair. Do not plunge into it without due reflection. I myself am a husband, and, though singularly blessed in the possession of a devoted helpmeet, cannot but feel sometimes that a man is better off as a bachelor. Women, Mulliner, are odd.'

'True,' said Augustine.

'My own dear wife is the best of women. And, as I never weary of saying, a good woman is a wondrous creature, cleaving to the right and the good under all change; lovely in youthful comeliness, lovely all her life in comeliness of heart. And yet—'

'And yet?' said Augustine.

The bishop mused for a moment. He wriggled a little with an expression of pain, and scratched himself between the shoulder-blades.

'Well, I'll tell you,' said the bishop. 'It is a warm and pleasant day to-day, is it not?'

'Exceptionally clement,' said Augustine.

'A fair, sunny day, made gracious by a temperate westerly breeze. And yet, Mulliner, if you will credit my statement, my wife insisted on my putting on my thick winter woollies this morning. Truly,' sighed the bishop, 'as a jewel of gold in a swine's snout, so is a fair woman which is without discretion. Proverbs xi. 21.'

'Twenty-two,' corrected Augustine.

'I should have said twenty-two. They are made of thick flannel, and I have an exceptionally sensitive skin. Oblige me, my dear fellow, by rubbing me in the small of the back with the ferrule of your stick. I think it will ease the irritation.'

'But, my poor dear old bish,' said Augustine, sympathetically, 'this must not be.'

The bishop shook his head ruefully.

'You would not speak so hardily, Mulliner, if you knew my wife. There is no appeal from her decrees.'

'Nonsense,' cried Augustine, cheerily. He looked through the trees to where the lady bishopess, escorted by Jane, was examining a lobelia through her lorgnette with just the right blend of cordiality and condescension. 'I'll fix that for you in a second.'

The bishop clutched at his arm.

'My boy! What are you going to do?'

'I'm just going to have a word with your wife and put the matter up to her as a reasonable woman. Thick winter woollies on a day like this! Absurd!' said Augustine. 'Preposterous! I never heard such rot.'

The bishop gazed after him with a laden heart. Already he had come to love this young man like a son: and to see him charging so light-heartedly into the very jaws of destruction afflicted him with a deep and poignant sadness. He knew what his wife was like when even the highest in the land attempted to thwart her; and this brave lad was but a curate. In another moment she would be looking at him through her lorgnette: and England was littered with the shrivelled remains of curates at whom the lady bishopess had looked through her lorgnette. He had seen them wilt like salted slugs at the episcopal breakfast-table.

He held his breath. Augustine had reached the lady bishopess, and the lady bishopess was even now raising her lorgnette.

The bishop shut his eyes and turned away. And then – years afterwards, it seemed to him – a cheery voice hailed him: and, turning, he perceived Augustine bounding back through the trees.

'It's all right, bish,' said Augustine.

'All – all right?' faltered the bishop.

'Yes. She says you can go and change into the thin cashmere.'

The bishop reeled.

'But – but – but what did you say to her? What arguments did you employ?'

'Oh, I just pointed out what a warm day it was and jollied her along a bit—'

'Jollied her along a bit!'

'And she agreed in the most friendly and cordial manner. She has asked me to call at the Palace one of these days.'

The bishop seized Augustine's hand.

'My boy,' he said in a broken voice, 'you shall do more than call at the Palace. You shall come and live at the Palace. Become my secretary, Mulliner, and name your own salary. If you intend to marry, you will require an increased stipend. Become my secretary, boy, and never leave my side. I have needed somebody like you for years.'

It was late in the afternoon when Augustine returned to his rooms, for he had been invited to lunch at the vicarage and had been the life and soul of the cheery little party.

'A letter for you, sir,' said Mrs Wardle, obsequiously.

Augustine took the letter.

'I am sorry to say I shall be leaving you shortly, Mrs Wardle.'

'Oh, sir! If there's anything I can do—'

'Oh, it's not that. The fact is, the bishop has made me his secretary, and I shall have to shift my toothbrush and spats to the Palace, you see.'

'Well, fancy that, sir! Why, you'll be a bishop yourself one of these days.'

'Possibly,' said Augustine. 'Possibly. And now let me read this.'

He opened the letter. A thoughtful frown appeared on his face as he read.

My dear Augustine,

I am writing in some haste to tell you that the impulsiveness of your aunt has led to a rather serious mistake.

She tells me that she dispatched to you yesterday by parcels post a sample bottle of my new Buck-U-Uppo, which she obtained without my knowledge from my laboratory. Had she mentioned what she was intending to do, I could have prevented a very unfortunate occurrence.

Mulliner's Buck-U-Uppo is of two grades or qualities – the A and the B. The A is a mild, but strengthening, tonic designed for human invalids. The B, on the other hand, is purely for circulation in the animal kingdom, and was invented to fill a long-felt want throughout our Indian possessions.

As you are doubtless aware, the favourite pastime of the Indian Maharajahs is the hunting of the tiger of the jungle from the backs of elephants; and it has happened frequently in the past that hunts have been spoiled by the failure of the elephant to see eye to eye with its owner in the matter of what constitutes sport.

Too often elephants, on sighting the tiger, have turned and galloped home: and it was to correct this tendency on their part that I invented Mulliner's Buck-U-Uppo 'B'. One teaspoonful of the Buck-U-Uppo 'B' administered in its morning bran-mash will cause the most timid elephant to trumpet loudly and charge the fiercest tiger without a qualm.

Abstain, therefore, from taking any of the contents of the bottle you now possess,

And believe me,

Your affectionate uncle,

Wilfred Mulliner.

Augustine remained for some time in deep thought after perusing this communication. Then, rising, he whistled a few bars of the psalm appointed for the twenty-sixth of June and left the room.

Half an hour later a telegraphic message was speeding over the wires.

It ran as follows: –

Wilfred Mulliner,
The Gables,
Lesser Lossingham,
Salop.

Letter received. Send immediately, C.O.D., three cases of the 'B'. 'Blessed shall be thy basket and thy store.' Deuteronomy xxviii. 5.

Augustine.

THE SPOT OF ART

I was lunching at my Aunt Dahlia's, and despite the fact that Anatole, her outstanding cook, had rather excelled himself in the matter of the bill-of-fare, I'm bound to say the food was more or less turning to ashes in my mouth. You see, I had some bad news to break to her – always a prospect that takes the edge off the appetite. She wouldn't be pleased, I knew, and when not pleased Aunt Dahlia, having spent most of her youth in the hunting-field, has a crispish way of expressing herself.

However, I supposed I had better have a dash at it and get it over.

'Aunt Dahlia,' I said, facing the issue squarely.

'Hullo?'

'You know that cruise of yours?'

'Yes.'

'That yachting-cruise you are planning?'

'Yes.'

'That jolly cruise in your yacht in the Mediterranean

to which you so kindly invited me and to which I have been looking forward with such keen anticipation?'

'Get on, fathead, what about it?'

I swallowed a chunk of *cotelette-suprême-aux-choux-fleurs* and slipped her the distressing info'.

'I'm frightfully sorry, Aunt Dahlia,' I said, 'but I shan't be able to come.'

As I had foreseen, she goggled.

'What!'

'I'm afraid not.'

'You poor, miserable hell-hound, what do you mean, you won't be able to come?'

'Well, I won't.'

'Why not?'

'Matters of the most extreme urgency render my presence in the Metropolis imperative.'

She sniffed.

'I suppose what you really mean is that you're hanging round some unfortunate girl again?'

I didn't like the way she put it, but I admit I was stunned by her penetration, if that's the word I want. I mean the sort of thing detectives have.

'Yes, Aunt Dahlia,' I said, 'you have guessed my secret. I do indeed love.'

'Who is she?'

'A Miss Pendlebury. Christian name, Gwladys. She spells it with a "w".'

'With a "g", you mean.'

'With a "w" *and* a "g".'

'Not Gwladys?'

'That's it.'

The relative uttered a yowl.

'You sit there and tell me you haven't enough sense to steer clear of a girl who calls herself Gwladys? Listen, Bertie,' said Aunt Dahlia earnestly, 'I'm an older woman than you are – well, you know what I mean – and I can tell you a thing or two. And one of them is that no good can come of association with anything labelled Gwladys or Ysobel or Ethyl or Mabelle or Kathryn. But particularly Gwladys. What sort of girl is she?'

'Slightly divine.'

'She isn't that female I saw driving you at sixty miles p.h. in the Park the other day. In a red two-seater?'

'She did drive me in the Park the other day. I thought it rather a hopeful sign. And her Widgeon Seven is red.'

Aunt Dahlia looked relieved.

'Oh well, then, she'll probably break your silly fat neck before she can get you to the altar. That's some consolation. Where did you meet her?'

'At a party in Chelsea. She's an artist.'

'Ye gods!'

'And swings a jolly fine brush, let me tell you. She's painted a portrait of me. Jeeves and I hung it up in the flat this morning. I have an idea Jeeves doesn't like it.'

'Well, if it's anything like you I don't see why he should. An artist! Calls herself Gwladys! And drives a car in the sort of way Segrave would if he were pressed for time.' She brooded awhile. 'Well, it's all very sad, but I can't see why you won't come on the yacht.'

I explained.

'It would be madness to leave the metrop. at this juncture,' I said. 'You know what girls are. They forget the absent face. And I'm not at all easy in my mind about a certain cove of the name of Lucius Pim. Apart from the fact that he's an artist, too, which forms a bond, his hair waves. One must never discount wavy hair, Aunt Dahlia. Moreover, this bloke is one of those strong, masterful men. He treats Gwladys as if she were less than the dust beneath his taxi wheels. He criticizes her hats and says nasty things about her chiaroscuro. For some reason, I've often noticed, this always seems to fascinate girls, and it has sometimes occurred to me that, being myself more the parfait gentle knight, if you know what I mean, I am in grave danger of getting the short end. Taking all these things into consideration, then, I cannot breeze off to the Mediterranean, leaving this Pim a clear field. You must see that?'

Aunt Dahlia laughed. Rather a nasty laugh. Scorn in its *timbre*, or so it seemed to me.

'I shouldn't worry,' she said. 'You don't suppose for a moment that Jeeves will sanction the match?'

I was stung.

'Do you imply, Aunt Dahlia,' I said – and I can't remember if I rapped the table with the handle of my fork or not, but I rather think I did – 'that I allow Jeeves to boss me to the extent of stopping me marrying somebody I want to marry?'

'Well, he stopped you wearing a moustache, didn't he? And purple socks. And soft-fronted shirts with dress-clothes.'

'That is a different matter altogether.'

'Well, I'm prepared to make a small bet with you, Bertie. Jeeves will stop this match.'

'What absolute rot!'

'And if he doesn't like that portrait, he will get rid of it.'

'I never heard such dashed nonsense in my life.'

'And, finally, you wretched, pie-faced wambler, he will present you on board my yacht at the appointed hour. I don't know how he will do it, but you will be there, all complete with yachting-cap and spare pair of socks.'

'Let us change the subject, Aunt Dahlia,' I said coldly.

Being a good deal stirred up by the attitude of the flesh-and-blood at the luncheon-table, I had to go for a bit of a walk in the Park after leaving, to soothe the nervous system. By about four-thirty the ganglions had ceased to vibrate, and I returned to the flat. Jeeves was in the sitting-room, looking at the portrait.

I felt a trifle embarrassed in the man's presence, because just before leaving I had informed him of my intention to scratch the yacht-trip, and he had taken it on the chin a bit. You see, he had been looking forward to it rather. From the moment I had accepted the invitation, there had been a sort of nautical glitter in his eye, and I'm not sure I hadn't heard him trolling Chanties in the kitchen. I think some ancestor of his must have been one of Nelson's tars or something, for he has always had the urge of the salt sea in his blood. I have noticed him on liners, when we were going to America, striding the deck with a sailorly roll and giving the distinct impression of being just about to heave the main-brace or splice the binnacle.

So, though I had explained my reasons, taking the man fully into my confidence and concealing nothing, I knew that he was distinctly peeved; and my first act, on entering, was to do the cheery a bit. I joined him in front of the portrait.

'Looks good, Jeeves, what?'

'Yes, sir.'

'Nothing like a spot of art for brightening the home.'

'No, sir.'

'Seems to lend the room a certain – what shall I say—'

'Yes, sir.'

The responses were all right, but his manner was far from hearty, and I decided to tackle him squarely. I mean, dash it. I mean, I don't know if you have ever had your portrait painted, but if you have you will understand my feelings. The spectacle of one's portrait hanging on the wall creates in one a sort of paternal fondness for the thing: and what you demand from the outside public is approval and enthusiasm – not the curling lip, the twitching nostril, and the kind of supercilious look which you see in the eye of a dead mackerel. Especially is this so when the artist is a girl for whom you have conceived sentiments deeper and warmer than those of ordinary friendship.

'Jeeves,' I said, 'you don't like this spot of art.'

'Oh, yes, sir.'

'No. Subterfuge is useless. I can read you like a book. For some reason this spot of art fails to appeal to you. What do you object to about it?'

'Is not the colour-scheme a trifle bright, sir?'

'I had not observed it, Jeeves. Anything else?'

'Well, in my opinion, sir, Miss Pendlebury has given you a somewhat too hungry expression.'

'Hungry?'

'A little like that of a dog regarding a distant bone, sir.'

I checked the fellow.

'There is no resemblance whatever, Jeeves, to a dog regarding a distant bone. The look to which you allude is wistful and denotes Soul.'

'I see, sir.'

I proceeded to another subject.

'Miss Pendlebury said she might look in this afternoon to inspect the portrait. Did she turn up?'

'Yes, sir.'

'But has left?'

'Yes, sir.'

'You mean she's gone, what?'

'Precisely, sir.'

'She didn't say anything about coming back, I suppose?'

'No, sir. I received the impression that it was not Miss Pendlebury's intention to return. She was a little upset, sir, and expressed a desire to go to her studio and rest.'

'Upset? What was she upset about?'

'The accident, sir.'

I didn't actually clutch the brow, but I did a bit of mental brow-clutching, as it were.

'Don't tell me she had an accident!'

'Yes, sir.'

'What sort of accident?'

'Automobile, sir.'

'Was she hurt?'

'No, sir. Only the gentleman.'

'What gentleman?'

'Miss Pendlebury had the misfortune to run over a gentleman in her car almost immediately opposite this building. He sustained a slight fracture of the leg.'

'Too bad! But Miss Pendlebury is all right?'

'Physically, sir, her condition appeared to be satisfactory. She was suffering a certain distress of mind.'

'Of course, with her beautiful, sympathetic nature. Naturally. It's a hard world for a girl, Jeeves, with fellows flinging themselves under the wheels of her car in one long, unending stream. It must have been a great shock to her. What became of the chump?'

'The gentleman, sir?'

'Yes.'

'He is in your spare bedroom, sir.'

'What!'

'Yes, sir.'

'In my spare bedroom?'

'Yes, sir. It was Miss Pendlebury's desire that he should be taken there. She instructed me to telegraph to the gentleman's sister, sir, who is in Paris, advising her of the accident. I also summoned a medical man, who gave it as his opinion that the patient should remain for the time being *in statu quo*.'

'You mean, the corpse is on the premises for an indefinite visit?'

'Yes, sir.'

'Jeeves, this is a bit thick!'

'Yes, sir.'

And I meant it, dash it. I mean to say, a girl can be pretty heftily divine and ensnare the heart and what not, but she's no right to turn a fellow's flat into a morgue. I'm bound to say that for a moment passion ebbed a trifle.

'Well, I suppose I'd better go and introduce myself to the blighter. After all, I am his host. Has he a name?'

'Mr Pim, sir.'

'Pim!'

'Yes, sir. And the young lady addressed him as Lucius. It was owing to the fact that he was on his way here to examine the portrait which she had painted that Mr Pim happened to be in the roadway at the moment when Miss Pendlebury turned the corner.'

I headed for the spare bedroom. I was perturbed to a degree. I don't know if you have ever loved and been handicapped in your wooing by a wavy-haired rival, but one of the things you don't want in such circs is the rival parking himself on the premises with a broken leg. Apart from anything else, the advantage the position gives him is obviously terrific. There he is, sitting up and toying with a grape and looking pale and interesting, the object of the girl's pity and concern, and where do you get off, bounding about the place in morning costume and spats and with the rude flush of health on the cheek? It seemed to me that things were beginning to look pretty mouldy.

I found Lucius Pim lying in bed, draped in a suit of my pyjamas, smoking one of my cigarettes, and reading a detective story. He waved the cigarette at me in what I considered a dashed patronizing manner.

'Ah, Wooster!' he said.

'Not so much of the "Ah, Wooster!"' I replied brusquely. 'How soon can you be moved?'

'In a week or so, I fancy.'

'In a week!'

'Or so. For the moment, the doctor insists on perfect quiet and repose. So forgive me, old man, for asking you not to raise your voice. A hushed whisper is the stuff to give the troops. And now, Wooster, about this accident. We must come to an understanding.'

'Are you sure you can't be moved?'

'Quite. The doctor said so.'

'I think we ought to get a second opinion.'

'Useless, my dear fellow. He was most emphatic, and evidently a man who knew his job. Don't worry about my not being comfortable here. I shall be quite all right. I like this bed. And now, to return to the subject of this accident. My sister will be arriving to-morrow. She will be greatly upset. I am her favourite brother.'

'You are?'

'I am.'

'How many of you are there?'

'Six.'

'And you're her favourite?'

'I am.'

It seemed to me that the other five must be pretty fairly sub-human, but I didn't say so. We Woosters can curb the tongue.

'She married a bird named Slingsby. Slingsby's Superb Soups. He rolls in money. But do you think I can get him to lend a trifle from time to time to a needy brother-in-law?' said Lucius Pim bitterly. 'No, sir! However, that is neither here nor there. The point is that my sister loves me devotedly: and, this being the case, she might try to prosecute and persecute and generally bite pieces out of poor little Gwladys if she knew that it was she who was driving the car that laid me out. She must never know, Wooster. I appeal to you as a man of honour to keep your mouth shut.'

'Naturally.'

'I'm glad you grasp the point so readily, Wooster. You are not the fool people take you for.'

'Who takes me for a fool?'

The Pim raised his eyebrows slightly.

'Don't people?' he said. 'Well, well. Anyway, that's settled. Unless I can think of something better I shall tell my sister that I was knocked down by a car which drove on without stopping and I didn't get its number. And now perhaps you had better leave me. The doctor made a point of quiet and repose. Moreover, I want to go on with this story. The villain has just dropped a cobra down the heroine's chimney, and I must be at her side. It is impossible not to be thrilled by Edgar Wallace. I'll ring if I want anything.'

I headed for the sitting-room. I found Jeeves there, staring at the portrait in rather a marked manner, as if it hurt him.

'Jeeves,' I said, 'Mr Pim appears to be a fixture.'

'Yes, sir.'

'For the nonce, at any rate. And to-morrow we shall have his sister, Mrs Slingsby, of Slingsby's Superb Soups, in our midst.'

'Yes, sir. I telegraphed to Mrs Slingsby shortly before four. Assuming her to have been at her hotel in Paris at the moment of the telegram's delivery, she will no doubt take a boat early to-morrow afternoon, reaching Dover – or, should she prefer the alternative route, Folkestone – in time to begin the railway journey at an hour which will enable her to arrive in London at about seven. She will possibly proceed first to her London residence—'

'Yes, Jeeves,' I said, 'yes. A gripping story, full of action and human interest. You must have it set to music some time and sing it. Meanwhile, get this into your head. It is imperative that Mrs Slingsby does not learn that it was Miss Pendlebury who broke her brother in two places. I shall require you, therefore, to approach Mr Pim before she arrives, ascertain exactly what tale he intends to tell, and be prepared to back it up in every particular.'

'Very good, sir.'

'And now, Jeeves, what of Miss Pendlebury?'

'Sir?'

'She's sure to call to make enquiries.'

'Yes, sir.'

'Well, she mustn't find me here. You know all about women, Jeeves?'

'Yes, sir.'

'Then tell me this. Am I not right in supposing that if Miss Pendlebury is in a position to go into the sick-room, take a long look at the interesting invalid, and then pop out, with the memory of that look fresh in her mind, and get a square sight of me lounging about in sponge-bag trousers, she will draw damaging comparisons? You see what I mean? Look on this picture and on that – the one romantic, the other not . . . Eh?'

'Very true, sir. It is a point which I had intended to bring to your attention. An invalid undoubtedly exercises a powerful appeal to the motherliness which exists in every woman's heart, sir. Invalids seem to stir their deepest feelings. The poet Scott has put the matter neatly in the lines – "Oh, Woman in our hours of ease uncertain, coy, and hard to please . . . When pain and anguish rack the brow—"'

I held up a hand.

'At some other time, Jeeves,' I said, 'I shall be delighted to hear you say your piece, but just now I am not in the mood. The position being as I have outlined, I propose to clear out early to-morrow morning and not to reappear until nightfall. I shall take the car and dash down to Brighton for the day.'

'Very good, sir.'

'It is better so, is it not, Jeeves?'

'Indubitably, sir.'

'I think so, too. The sea breezes will tone up my system, which sadly needs a dollop of toning. I leave you in charge of the old home.'

'Very good, sir.'

'Convey my regrets and sympathy to Miss Pendlebury and tell her I have been called away on business.'

'Yes, sir.'

'Should the Slingsby require refreshment, feed her in moderation.'

'Very good, sir.'

'And, in poisoning Mr Pim's soup, don't use arsenic,

which is readily detected. Go to a good chemist and get something that leaves no traces.'

I sighed, and cocked an eye at the portrait.

'All this is very wonky, Jeeves.'

'Yes, sir.'

'When that portrait was painted, I was a happy man.'

'Yes, sir.'

'Ah, well, Jeeves!'

'Very true, sir.'

And we left it at that.

It was lateish when I got back on the following evening. What with a bit of ozone-sniffing, a good dinner, and a nice run home in the moonlight with the old car going as sweet as a nut, I was feeling in pretty good shape once more. In fact, coming through Purley, I went so far as to sing a trifle. The spirit of the Woosters is a buoyant spirit, and optimism had begun to reign again in the W. bosom.

The way I looked at it was, I saw I had been mistaken in assuming that a girl must necessarily love a fellow just because he has broken a leg. At first, no doubt, Gwladys Pendlebury would feel strangely drawn to the Pim when she saw him lying there a more or less total loss. But it would not be long before other reflections crept in. She would ask herself if she were wise in trusting her life's happiness to a man who hadn't enough sense to leap out of the way when he saw a car coming. She would tell herself that, if this sort of thing had happened once, who knew that it might not go on happening again and again all down the long years. And she would recoil from a married life which consisted entirely of going to hospitals and taking her husband fruit. She would realize how much better off she would be, teamed up with a fellow like Bertram Wooster, who, whatever his faults, at least walked on the pavement and looked up and down a street before he crossed it.

It was in excellent spirits, accordingly, that I put the car in the garage, and it was with a merry Tra-la on my lips that I let myself into the flat as Big Ben began to strike eleven. I rang the bell and presently, as if he had divined my wishes, Jeeves came in with siphon and decanter.

'Home again, Jeeves,' I said, mixing a spot.

'Yes, sir.'

'What has been happening in my absence? Did Miss Pendlebury call?'

'Yes, sir. At about two o'clock.'

'And left?'

'At about six, sir.'

I didn't like this so much. A four-hour visit struck me as a bit sinister. However, there was nothing to be done about it.

'And Mrs Slingsby?'

'She arrived shortly after eight and left at ten, sir.'

'Ah? Agitated?'

'Yes, sir. Particularly when she left. She was very desirous of seeing you, sir.'

'Seeing me?'

'Yes, sir.'

'Wanted to thank me brokenly, I suppose, for so courteously allowing her favourite brother a place to have his game legs in. Eh?'

'Possibly, sir. On the other hand, she alluded to you in terms suggestive of disapprobation, sir.'

'She – what?'

'"Feckless idiot" was one of the expressions she employed, sir.'

'Feckless idiot?'

'Yes, sir.'

I couldn't make it out. I simply couldn't see what the woman had based her judgement on. My Aunt Agatha has frequently said that sort of thing about me, but she has known me from a boy.

'I must look into this, Jeeves. Is Mr Pim asleep?'

'No, sir. He rang the bell a moment ago to enquire if we had not a better brand of cigarette in the flat.'

'He did, did he?'

'Yes, sir.'

'The accident doesn't seem to have affected his nerve.'

'No, sir.'

I found Lucius Pim sitting propped up among the pillows, reading his detective story.

'Ah, Wooster,' he said. 'Welcome home. I say, in case you were worrying, it's all right about that cobra. The hero had got at it without the villain's knowledge and extracted its poison-fangs. With the result that when it fell down the chimney and started trying to bite the heroine its efforts were null and void. I doubt if a cobra has ever felt so silly.'

'Never mind about cobras.'

'It's no good saying "Never mind about cobras",' said Lucius Pim in a gentle, rebuking sort of voice. 'You've jolly well *got* to mind about cobras, if they haven't had their poison-fangs extracted. Ask anyone. By the way, my sister looked in. She wants to have a word with you.'

'And I want to have a word with her.'

'"Two minds with but a single thought". What she wants to talk to you about is this accident of mine. You remember that story I was to tell her? About the car driving on? Well the understanding was, if you recollect, that I was only to tell it if I couldn't think of something better. Fortunately, I thought of something much better. It came to me in a flash as I lay in bed looking at the ceiling. You see, that driving-on story was thin. People don't knock fellows down and break their legs and go driving on. The thing wouldn't have held water for a minute. So I told her you did it.'

'What!'

'I said it was you who did it in your car. Much more likely. Makes the whole thing neat and well-rounded. I knew you would approve. At all costs we have got to keep it from her that I was outed by Gwladys. I made it as easy for you as I could, saying that you were a bit pickled at the time and so not to be blamed for what you did. Some fellows wouldn't have thought of that. Still,' said Lucius Pim with a sigh, 'I'm afraid she's not any too pleased with you.'

'She isn't, isn't she?'

'No, she is not. And I strongly recommend you, if you want anything like a pleasant interview to-morrow, to sweeten her a bit overnight.'

'How do you mean, sweeten her?'

'I'd suggest you sent her some flowers. It would be a graceful gesture. Roses are her favourites. Shoot her in a few roses – Number Three, Hill Street is the address – and it may make all the difference. I think it my duty to inform you, old man, that my sister Beatrice is rather a tough egg, when roused. My brother-in-law is due back from New York at any moment, and the danger, as I see it, is that Beatrice, unless sweetened, will get at him and make him bring actions against you for torts and malfeasances and what not and get thumping damages. He isn't over-fond of me and, left to himself, would rather approve than otherwise of people who broke my legs: but he's crazy about Beatrice and will do anything she asks him to. So my advice is, Gather ye rose-buds, while ye may and bung them in to Number Three, Hill Street. Otherwise, the case of Slingsby *v.* Wooster will be on the calendar before you can say "What-ho".'

I gave the fellow a look. Lost on him, of course.

'It's a pity you didn't think of all that before,' I said. And it wasn't so much the actual words, if you know what I mean, as the way I said it.

'I thought of it all right,' said Lucius Pim. 'But, as we were both agreed that at all costs—'

'Oh, all right,' I said. 'All right, all right.'

'You aren't annoyed?' said Lucius Pim, looking at me with a touch of surprise.

'Oh, no!'

'Splendid,' said Lucius Pim, relieved. 'I knew you would feel that I had done the only possible thing. It would have been awful if Beatrice had found out about Gwladys. I daresay you have noticed, Wooster, that when women find themselves in a position to take a running kick at one of their own sex they are twice as rough on her as they would be on a man. Now, you, being of the male persuasion, will find everything made nice and smooth for you. A quart of assorted roses, a few smiles, a tactful word or two, and she'll have melted before you know where you are. Play your cards properly, and you and Beatrice will be laughing merrily and having a game of Round and Round the Mulberry Bush together in about five minutes. Better not let Slingsby's Soups catch you at it, however. He's very jealous where Beatrice is concerned. And now you'll forgive me, old chap, if I send you away. The doctor says I ought not to talk too much for a day or two. Besides, it's time for bye-bye.'

The more I thought it over, the better that idea of sending those roses looked. Lucius Pim was not a man I was fond of – in fact, if I had had to choose between him and a cockroach as a companion for a walking-tour, the cockroach would have had it by a short head – but there was no doubt that he had outlined the right policy. His advice was good, and I decided to follow it. Rising next morning at ten-fifteen, I swallowed a strengthening breakfast and legged it off to that flower-shop in Piccadilly. I couldn't leave the thing to Jeeves. It was essentially a mission that demanded the personal touch. I laid out a couple of quid on a sizeable bouquet, sent it with my card to Hill Street, and then looked in at the Drones for a brief refresher. It is a thing I don't often do in the morning, but this threatened to be rather a special morning.

It was about noon when I got back to the flat. I went into the sitting-room and tried to adjust the mind to the coming interview. It had to be faced, of course, but it wasn't any good my telling myself that it was going to be one of those jolly scenes the memory of which cheer you up as you sit toasting your toes at the fire in your old age. I stood or fell by the roses. If they sweetened the Slingsby, all would be well. If they failed to sweeten her, Bertram was undoubtedly for it.

The clock ticked on, but she did not come. A late riser, I took it, and was slightly encouraged by the reflection. My experience of women has been that the earlier they leave the hay the more vicious specimens they are apt to be. My Aunt Agatha, for instance, is always up with the lark, and look at her.

Still, you couldn't be sure that this rule always worked, and after a while the suspense began to get in amongst me a bit. To divert the mind, I fetched the old putter out of its bag and began to practise putts into a glass. After all, even if the Slingsby turned out to be all that I had pictured her in my gloomier moments, I should have improved my close-to-the-hole work on the green and be that much up, at any rate.

It was while I was shaping for a rather tricky shot that the front-door bell went.

I picked up the glass and shoved the putter behind the settee. It struck me that if the woman found me engaged on what you might call a frivolous pursuit she might take it to indicate lack of remorse and proper feeling. I straightened the collar, pulled down the waistcoat, and managed to fasten on the face a sort of sad half-smile which was welcoming without being actually jovial. It looked all right in the mirror, and I held it as the door opened.

'Mr Slingsby,' announced Jeeves.

And, having spoken these words, he closed the door and left us alone together.

For quite a time there wasn't anything in the way of chit-chat. The shock of expecting Mrs Slingsby and finding myself confronted by something entirely different – in fact, not the same thing at all – seemed to have affected the vocal cords. And the visitor didn't appear to be disposed to make light conversation himself. He stood there looking strong and silent. I suppose you have to be like that if you want to manufacture anything in the nature of a really convincing soup.

Slingsby's Superb Soups was a Roman Emperor-looking sort of bird, with keen, penetrating eyes and one of those jutting chins. The eyes seemed to be fixed on me in a dashed unpleasant stare and, unless I was mistaken, he was grinding his teeth a trifle. For some reason he appeared to have taken a strong dislike to me at sight, and I'm bound to say this rather puzzled me. I don't pretend to have one of those Fascinating Personalities which you get from studying the booklets advertised in the back pages of the magazines, but I couldn't recall another case in the whole of my career where a single glimpse of the old map had been enough to make anyone look as if he wanted to foam at the mouth. Usually, when people meet me for the first time, they don't seem to know I'm there.

However, I exerted myself to play the host.

'Mr Slingsby?'

'That is my name.'

'Just got back from America?'

'I landed this morning.'

'Sooner than you were expected, what?'

'So I imagine.'

'Very glad to see you.'

'You will not be long.'

I took time off to do a bit of gulping. I saw now what had happened. This bloke had been home, seen his wife, heard the story of the accident, and had hastened round to the flat to slip it across me. Evidently those roses had not sweetened the female of the species. The only thing to do now seemed to be to take a stab at sweetening the male.

'Have a drink?' I said.

'No!'

'A cigarette?'

'No!'

'A chair?'

'No!'

I went into the silence once more. These non-drinking, non-smoking non-sitters are hard birds to handle.

'Don't grin at me, sir!'

I shot a glance at myself in the mirror, and saw what he meant. The sad half-smile *had* slopped over a bit. I adjusted it, and there was another pause.

'Now, sir,' said the Superb Souper. 'To business. I think I need scarcely tell you why I am here.'

'No. Of course. Absolutely. It's about that little matter—'

He gave a snort which nearly upset a vase on the mantelpiece.

'Little matter? So you consider it a little matter, do you?'

'Well—'

'Let me tell you, sir, that when I find that during my absence from the country a man has been annoying my wife with his importunities I regard it as anything but a little matter. And I shall endeavour,' said the Souper, the eyes gleaming a trifle brighter as he rubbed his hands together in a hideous, menacing way, 'to make you see the thing in the same light.'

I couldn't make head or tail of this. I simply couldn't follow him. The lemon began to swim.

'Eh?' I said. 'Your wife?'

'You heard me.'

'There must be some mistake.'

'There is. You made it.'

'But I don't know your wife.'

'Ha!'

'I've never even met her.'

'Tchah!'

'Honestly, I haven't.'

'Bah!'

He drank me in for a moment.

'Do you deny you sent her flowers?'

I felt the heart turn a double somersault. I began to catch his drift.

'Flowers!' he proceeded. 'Roses, sir. Great, fat, beastly roses. Enough of them to sink a ship. Your card was attached to them by a small pin—'

His voice died away in a sort of gurgle, and I saw that he was staring at something behind me. I spun round, and there, in the doorway – I hadn't seen it open, because during the last spasm of dialogue I had been backing cautiously towards it – there in the doorway stood a female. One glance was enough to tell me who she was. No woman could look so like Lucius Pim who hadn't the misfortune to be related to him. It was Sister Beatrice, the tough egg.

I saw all. She had left home before the flowers had arrived: she had sneaked, unsweetened, into the flat, while I was fortifying the system at the Drones: and here she was.

'Er—' I said.

'Alexander!' said the female.

'Goo!' said the Souper. Or it may have been 'Coo'.

Whatever it was, it was in the nature of a battle-cry or slogan of war. The Souper's worst suspicions had obviously been confirmed. His eyes shone with a strange light. His chin pushed itself out another couple of inches. He clenched and unclenched his fingers once or twice, as if to make sure that they were working properly and could be relied on to do a good, clean job of strangling. Then, once more observing 'Coo!' (or 'Goo!'), he sprang forward, trod on the golf-ball I had been practising putting with, and took one of the finest tosses I have ever witnessed. The purler of a lifetime. For a moment the air seemed to be full of arms and legs, and then, with a thud that nearly dislocated the flat, he made a forced landing against the wall.

And, feeling I had had about all I wanted, I oiled from the room and was in the act of grabbing my hat from the rack in the hall, when Jeeves appeared.

'I fancied I heard a noise, sir,' said Jeeves.

'Quite possibly,' I said. 'It was Mr Slingsby.'

'Sir?'

'Mr Slingsby practising Russian dances,' I explained. 'I rather think he has fractured an assortment of limbs. Better go in and see.'

'Very good, sir.'

'If he is the wreck I imagine, put him in my room and send for the doctor. The flat is filling up nicely with the various units of the Pim family and its connections, eh, Jeeves?'

'Yes, sir.'

'I think the supply is about exhausted, but should any aunts or uncles by marriage come along and break their limbs, bed them out on the Chesterfield.'

'Very good, sir.'

'I, personally, Jeeves,' I said, opening the front door and pausing on the threshold, 'am off to Paris. I will wire you the address. Notify me in due course when the place is free from Pims and completely purged of Slingsbys, and I will return. Oh, and Jeeves.'

'Sir?'

'Spare no effort to mollify these birds. They think – at least, Slingsby (female) thinks, and what she thinks to-day he will think to-morrow – that it was I who ran over Mr Pim in my car. Endeavour during my absence to sweeten them.'

'Very good, sir.'

'And now perhaps you had better be going in and viewing the body. I shall proceed to the Drones, where I shall lunch, subsequently catching the two o'clock train at Charing Cross. Meet me there with an assortment of luggage.'

It was a matter of three weeks or so before Jeeves sent me the 'All clear' signal. I spent the time pottering pretty perturbedly about Paris and environs. It is a city I am fairly fond of, but I was glad to be able to return to the old home. I hopped on to a passing aeroplane and a couple of hours later was bowling through Croydon on my way to the centre of things. It was somewhere down in the Sloane Square neighbourhood that I first caught sight of the posters.

A traffic block had occurred, and I was glancing idly this way and that, when suddenly my eye was caught by something that looked familiar. And then I saw what it was.

Pasted on a blank wall and measuring about a hundred feet each way was an enormous poster, mostly red and blue. At the top of it were the words:

SLINGSBY'S SUPERB SOUPS

and at the bottom:

SUCCULENT AND STRENGTHENING

And, in between, me. Yes, dash it, Bertram Wooster in person. A reproduction of the Pendlebury portrait, perfect in every detail.

It was the sort of thing to make a fellow's eyes flicker, and mine flickered. You might say a mist seemed to roll before them. Then it lifted, and I was able to get a good long look before the traffic moved on.

Of all the absolutely foul sights I have ever seen, this took the biscuit with ridiculous ease. The thing was a bally libel on the Wooster face, and yet it was as unmistakable as if it had had my name under it. I saw now what Jeeves had meant when he said that the portrait had given me a hungry look. In the poster this look had become one of bestial greed. There I sat absolutely slavering through a monocle about six inches in circumference at a plateful of soup, looking as if I hadn't had a meal for weeks. The whole thing seemed to take one straight away into a different and a dreadful world.

I woke from a species of trance or coma to find myself at the door of the block of flats. To buzz upstairs and charge into the home was with me the work of a moment.

Jeeves came shimmering down the hall, the respectful beam of welcome on his face.

'I am glad to see you back, sir.'

'Never mind about that,' I yipped. 'What about—?'

'The posters, sir? I was wondering if you might have observed them.'

'I observed them!'

'Striking, sir?'

'Very striking. Now, perhaps you'll kindly explain—'

'You instructed me, if you recollect, sir, to spare no effort to mollify Mr Slingsby.'

'Yes, but—'

'It proved a somewhat difficult task, sir. For some time Mr Slingsby, on the advice and owing to the persuasion of Mrs Slingsby, appeared to be resolved to institute an action in law against you – a procedure which I knew you would find most distasteful.'

'Yes, but—'

'And then, the first day he was able to leave his bed, he observed the portrait, and it seemed to me judicious to point out to him its possibilities as an advertising medium. He readily fell in with the suggestion and, on my assurance that, should he abandon the projected action in law, you would willingly permit the use of the portrait, he entered into negotiations with Miss Pendlebury for the purchase of the copyright.'

'Oh? Well, I hope she's got something out of it, at any rate?'

'Yes, sir. Mr Pim, acting as Miss Pendlebury's agent, drove, I understand, an extremely satisfactory bargain.'

'He acted as her agent, eh?'

'Yes, sir. In his capacity as fiancé to the young lady, sir.'

'Fiancé!'

'Yes, sir.'

It shows how the sight of that poster had got into my ribs when I state that, instead of being laid out cold by this announcement, I merely said 'Ha!' or 'Ho!' or it may have been 'H'm'. After the poster, nothing seemed to matter.

'After that poster, Jeeves,' I said, 'nothing seems to matter.'

'No, sir?'

'No, Jeeves. A woman has tossed my heart lightly away, but what of it?'

'Exactly, sir.'

'The voice of Love seemed to call to me, but it was a wrong number. Is that going to crush me?'

'No, sir.'

'No, Jeeves. It is not. But what does matter is this ghastly business of my face being spread from end to end of the Metropolis with the eyes fixed on a plate of Slingsby's Superb Soup. I must leave London. The lads at the Drones will kid me without ceasing.'

'Yes, sir. And Mrs Spenser Gregson—'

I paled visibly. I hadn't thought of Aunt Agatha and what she might have to say about letting down the family prestige.

'You don't mean to say she has been ringing up?'

'Several times daily, sir.'

'Jeeves, flight is the only resource.'

'Yes, sir.'

'Back to Paris, what?'

'I should not recommend the move, sir. The posters are, I understand, shortly to appear in that city also, advertising the *Bouillon Suprême*. Mr Slingsby's products command a large sale in France. The sight would be painful for you, sir.'

'Then where?'

'If I might make a suggestion, sir, why not adhere to your original intention of cruising in Mrs Travers' yacht in the Mediterranean? On the yacht you would be free from the annoyance of these advertising displays.'

The man seemed to me to be drivelling.

'But the yacht started weeks ago. It may be anywhere by now.'

'No, sir. The cruise was postponed for a month owing to the illness of Mr Travers' chef, Anatole, who contracted influenza. Mr Travers refused to sail without him.'

'You mean they haven't started?'

'Not yet, sir. The yacht sails from Southampton on Tuesday next.'

'Why, then, dash it, nothing could be sweeter.'

'No, sir.'

'Ring up Aunt Dahlia and tell her we'll be there.'

'I ventured to take the liberty of doing so a few moments before you arrived, sir.'

'You did?'

'Yes, sir. I thought it probable that the plan would meet with your approval.'

'It does! I've wished all along I was going on that cruise.'

'I, too, sir. It should be extremely pleasant.'

'The tang of the salt breezes, Jeeves!'

'Yes, sir.'

'The moonlight on the water!'

'Precisely, sir.'

'The gentle heaving of the waves!'

'Exactly, sir.'

I felt absolutely in the pink. Gwladys – pah! The posters – bah! That was the way I looked at it.

'Yo-ho-ho, Jeeves!' I said, giving the trousers a bit of a hitch.

'Yes, sir.'

'In fact, I will go further. Yo-ho-ho and a bottle of rum!'

'Very good, sir. I will bring it immediately.'

STRYCHNINE IN THE SOUP

From the moment the Draught Stout entered the bar-parlour of the Angler's Rest, it had been obvious that he was not his usual cheery self. His face was drawn and twisted, and he sat with bowed head in a distant corner by the window, contributing nothing to the conversation which, with Mr Mulliner as its centre, was in progress around the fire. From time to time he heaved a hollow sigh.

A sympathetic Lemonade and Angostura, putting down his glass, went across and laid a kindly hand on the sufferer's shoulder.

'What is it, old man?' he asked. 'Lost a friend?'

'Worse,' said the Draught Stout. 'A mystery novel. Got halfway through it on the journey down here, and left it in the train.'

'My nephew Cyril, the interior decorator,' said Mr Mulliner, 'once did the very same thing. These mental lapses are not infrequent.'

'And now,' proceeded the Draught Stout, 'I'm going

to have a sleepless night, wondering who poisoned Sir Geoffrey Tuttle, Bart.'

'The Bart was poisoned, was he?'

'You never said a truer word. Personally, I think it was the Vicar who did him in. He was known to be interested in strange poisons.'

Mr Mulliner smiled indulgently.

'It was not the Vicar,' he said. 'I happen to have read "The Murglow Manor Mystery". The guilty man was the plumber.'

'What plumber?'

'The one who comes in chapter two to mend the shower-bath. Sir Geoffrey had wronged his aunt in the year '96, so he fastened a snake in the nozzle of the shower-bath with glue; and when Sir Geoffrey turned on the stream the hot water melted the glue. This released the snake, which dropped through one of the holes, bit the Baronet in the leg, and disappeared down the waste-pipe.'

'But that can't be right,' said the Draught Stout. 'Between chapter two and the murder there was an interval of several days.'

'The plumber forgot his snake and had to go back for it,' explained Mr Mulliner. 'I trust that this revelation will prove sedative.'

'I feel a new man,' said the Draught Stout. 'I'd have lain awake worrying about that murder all night.'

'I suppose you would. My nephew Cyril was just the same. Nothing in this modern life of ours,' said Mr

Mulliner, taking a sip of his hot Scotch and lemon, 'is more remarkable than the way in which the mystery novel has gripped the public. Your true enthusiast, deprived of his favourite reading, will stop at nothing in order to get it. He is like a victim of the drug habit when withheld from cocaine. My nephew Cyril—'

'Amazing the things people will leave in trains,' said a Small Lager. 'Bags . . . umbrellas . . . even stuffed chimpanzees, occasionally, I've been told. I heard a story the other day—'

My nephew Cyril (said Mr Mulliner) had a greater passion for mystery stories than anyone I have ever met. I attribute this to the fact that, like so many interior decorators, he was a fragile, delicate young fellow, extraordinarily vulnerable to any ailment that happened to be going the rounds. Every time he caught mumps or influenza or German measles or the like, he occupied the period of convalescence in reading mystery stories. And, as the appetite grows by what it feeds on, he had become, at the time at which this narrative opens, a confirmed addict. Not only did he devour every volume of this type on which he could lay his hands, but he was also to be found at any theatre which was offering the kind of drama where skinny arms come unexpectedly out of the chiffonier and the audience feels a mild surprise if the lights stay on for ten consecutive minutes.

And it was during a performance of 'The Grey

Vampire' at the St James's that he found himself sitting next to Amelia Bassett, the girl whom he was to love with all the stored-up fervour of a man who hitherto had been inclined rather to edge away when in the presence of the other sex.

He did not know her name was Amelia Bassett. He had never seen her before. All he knew was that at last he had met his fate, and for the whole of the first act he was pondering the problem of how he was to make her acquaintance.

It was as the lights went up for the first intermission that he was aroused from his thoughts by a sharp pain in the right leg. He was just wondering whether it was gout or sciatica when, glancing down, he perceived that what had happened was that his neighbour, absorbed by the drama, had absent-mindedly collected a handful of his flesh and was twisting it in an ecstasy of excitement.

It seemed to Cyril a good *point d'appui*.

'Excuse me,' he said.

The girl turned. Her eyes were glowing, and the tip of her nose still quivered.

'I beg your pardon?'

'My leg,' said Cyril. 'Might I have it back, if you've finished with it?'

The girl looked down. She started visibly.

'I'm awfully sorry,' she gasped.

'Not at all,' said Cyril. 'Only too glad to have been of assistance.'

'I got carried away.'

'You are evidently fond of mystery plays.'

'I love them.'

'So do I. And mystery novels?'

'Oh, yes!'

'Have you read "Blood on the Banisters"?'

'Oh, *yes*! I thought it was better than "Severed Throats".'

'So did I,' said Cyril. 'Much better. Brighter murders, subtler detectives, crisper clues . . . better in every way.'

The two twin souls gazed into each other's eyes. There is no surer foundation for a beautiful friendship than a mutual taste in literature.

'My name is Amelia Bassett,' said the girl.

'Mine is Cyril Mulliner. Bassett?' He frowned thoughtfully. 'The name seems familiar.'

'Perhaps you have heard of my mother. Lady Bassett. She's rather a well-known big-game hunter and explorer. She tramps through jungles and things. She's gone out to the lobby for a smoke. By the way' – she hesitated – 'if she finds us talking, will you remember that we met at the Polterwoods'?'

'I quite understand.'

'You see, mother doesn't like people who talk to me without a formal introduction. And, when mother doesn't like anyone, she is so apt to hit them over the head with some hard instrument.'

'I see,' said Cyril. 'Like the Human Ape in "Gore by the Gallon".'

'Exactly. Tell me,' said the girl, changing the subject, 'if you were a millionaire, would you rather be stabbed in the back with a paper-knife or found dead without a mark on you, staring with blank eyes at some appalling sight?'

Cyril was about to reply when, looking past her, he found himself virtually in the latter position. A woman of extraordinary formidableness had lowered herself into the seat beyond and was scrutinizing him keenly through a tortoiseshell lorgnette. She reminded Cyril of Wallace Beery.

'Friend of yours, Amelia?' she said.

'This is Mr Mulliner, mother. We met at the Polterwoods'.'

'Ah?' said Lady Bassett.

She inspected Cyril through her lorgnette.

'Mr Mulliner,' she said, 'is a little like the chief of the Lower Isisi – though, of course, he was darker and had a ring through his nose. A dear, good fellow,' she continued reminiscently, 'but inclined to become familiar under the influence of trade gin. I shot him in the leg.'

'Er – why?' asked Cyril.

'He was not behaving like a gentleman,' said Lady Bassett primly.

'After taking your treatment,' said Cyril, awed, 'I'll bet he could have written a Book of Etiquette.'

'I believe he did,' said Lady Bassett carelessly. 'You must come and call on us some afternoon, Mr Mulliner.

I am in the telephone book. If you are interested in man-eating pumas, I can show you some nice heads.'

The curtain rose on act two, and Cyril returned to his thoughts. Love, he felt joyously, had come into his life at last. But then so, he had to admit, had Lady Bassett. There is, he reflected, always something.

I will pass lightly over the period of Cyril's wooing. Suffice it to say that his progress was rapid. From the moment he told Amelia that he had once met Dorothy Sayers, he never looked back. And one afternoon, calling and finding that Lady Bassett was away in the country, he took the girl's hand in his and told his love.

For a while all was well. Amelia's reactions proved satisfactory to a degree. She checked up enthusiastically on his proposition. Falling into his arms, she admitted specifically that he was her Dream Man.

Then came the jarring note.

'But it's no use,' she said, her lovely eyes filling with tears. 'Mother will never give her consent.'

'Why not?' said Cyril, stunned. 'What is it she objects to about me?'

'I don't know. But she generally alludes to you as "that pipsqueak".'

'Pipsqueak?' said Cyril. 'What *is* a pipsqueak?'

'I'm not quite sure, but it's something mother doesn't like very much. It's a pity she ever found out that you are an interior decorator.'

'An honourable profession,' said Cyril, a little stiffly.

'I know; but what she admires are men who have to do with the great open spaces.'

'Well, I also design ornamental gardens.'

'Yes,' said the girl doubtfully, 'but still—'

'And, dash it,' said Cyril indignantly, 'this isn't the Victorian age. All that business of Mother's Consent went out twenty years ago.'

'Yes, but no one told mother.'

'It's preposterous!' cried Cyril. 'I never heard such rot. Let's just slip off and get married quietly and send her a picture postcard from Venice or somewhere, with a cross and a "This is our room. Wish you were with us" on it.'

The girl shuddered.

'She would be with us,' she said. 'You don't know mother. The moment she got that picture postcard, she would come over to wherever we were and put you across her knee and spank you with a hair-brush. I don't think I could ever feel the same towards you if I saw you lying across mother's knee, being spanked with a hair-brush. It would spoil the honeymoon.'

Cyril frowned. But a man who has spent most of his life trying out a series of patent medicines is always an optimist.

'There is only one thing to be done,' he said. 'I shall see your mother and try to make her listen to reason. Where is she now?'

'She left this morning for a visit to the Winghams in Sussex.'

'Excellent! I know the Winghams. In fact, I have a standing invitation to go and stay with them whenever I like. I'll send them a wire and push down this evening. I will oil up to your mother sedulously and try to correct her present unfavourable impression of me. Then, choosing my moment, I will shoot her the news. It may work. It may not work. But at any rate I consider it a fair sporting venture.'

'But you are so diffident, Cyril. So shrinking. So retiring and shy. How can you carry through such a task?'

'Love will nerve me.'

'Enough, do you think? Remember what mother is. Wouldn't a good, strong drink be more help?'

Cyril looked doubtful.

'My doctor has always forbidden me alcoholic stimulants. He says they increase the blood pressure.'

'Well, when you meet mother, you will need all the blood pressure you can get. I really do advise you to fuel up a little before you see her.'

'Yes,' agreed Cyril, nodding thoughtfully. 'I think you're right. It shall be as you say. Good-bye, my angel one.'

'Good-bye, Cyril, darling. You will think of me every minute while you're gone?'

'Every single minute. Well, practically every single minute. You see, I have just got Horatio Slingsby's latest book, "Strychnine in the Soup", and I shall be dipping into that from time to time. But all the rest of the while . . . Have you read it, by the way?'

'Not yet. I had a copy, but mother took it with her.'

'Ah? Well, if I am to catch a train that will get me to Barkley for dinner, I must be going. Good-bye, sweetheart, and never forget that Gilbert Glendale in "The Missing Toe" won the girl he loved in spite of being up against two mysterious stranglers and the entire Black Moustache gang.'

He kissed her fondly, and went off to pack.

Barkley Towers, the country seat of Sir Mortimer and Lady Wingham, was two hours from London by rail. Thinking of Amelia and reading the opening chapters of Horatio Slingsby's powerful story, Cyril found the journey pass rapidly. In fact, so preoccupied was he that it was only as the train started to draw out of Barkley Regis station that he realized where he was. He managed to hurl himself on to the platform just in time.

As he had taken the five-seven express, stopping only at Gluebury Peveril, he arrived at Barkley Towers at an hour which enabled him not only to be on hand for dinner but also to take part in the life-giving distribution of cocktails which preceded the meal.

The house-party, he perceived on entering the drawing-room, was a small one. Besides Lady Bassett and himself, the only visitors were a nondescript couple of the name of Simpson, and a tall, bronzed, handsome man with flashing eyes who, his hostess informed him in a whispered aside, was Lester Mapledurham (pronounced Mum), the explorer and big-game hunter.

Perhaps it was the oppressive sensation of being in the same room with two explorers and big-game hunters that brought home to Cyril the need for following Amelia's advice as quickly as possible. But probably the mere sight of Lady Bassett alone would have been enough to make him break a lifelong abstinence. To her normal resemblance to Wallace Beery she appeared now to have added a distinct suggestion of Victor McLaglen, and the spectacle was sufficient to send Cyril leaping toward the cocktail tray.

After three rapid glasses he felt a better and a braver man. And so lavishly did he irrigate the ensuing dinner with hock, sherry, champagne, old brandy and port, that at the conclusion of the meal he was pleased to find that his diffidence had completely vanished. He rose from the table feeling equal to asking a dozen Lady Bassetts for their consent to marry a dozen daughters.

In fact, as he confided to the butler, prodding him genially in the ribs as he spoke, if Lady Bassett attempted to put on any dog with *him*, he would know what to do about it. He made no threats, he explained to the butler, he simply stated that he would know what to do about it. The butler said 'Very good, sir. Thank you, sir,' and the incident closed.

It had been Cyril's intention – feeling, as he did, in this singularly uplifted and dominant frame of mind – to get hold of Amelia's mother and start oiling up to her immediately after dinner. But, what with falling into a doze in the smoking-room and then getting into an argument on theology with one of the under-footmen whom he met in the hall, he did not reach the drawing-room until nearly half-past ten. And he was annoyed, on walking in with a merry cry of 'Lady Bassett! Call for Lady Bassett!' on his lips, to discover that she had retired to her room.

Had Cyril's mood been even slightly less elevated, this news might have acted as a check on his enthusiasm. So generous, however, had been Sir Mortimer's hospitality that he merely nodded eleven times, to indicate comprehension, and then, having ascertained that his quarry was roosting in the Blue Room, sped thither with a brief 'Tally-ho!'

Arriving at the Blue Room, he banged heartily on the door and breezed in. He found Lady Bassett propped up with pillows. She was smoking a cigar and reading a book. And that book, Cyril saw with intense surprise and resentment, was none other than Horatio Slingsby's 'Strychnine in the Soup'.

The spectacle brought him to an abrupt halt.

'Well, I'm dashed!' he cried. 'Well, I'm blowed! What do you mean by pinching my book?'

Lady Bassett had lowered her cigar. She now raised her eyebrows.

'What are you doing in my room, Mr Mulliner?'

'It's a little hard,' said Cyril, trembling with self-pity. 'I go to enormous expense to buy detective stories, and no sooner is my back turned than people rush about the place sneaking them.'

'This book belongs to my daughter Amelia.'

'Good old Amelia!' said Cyril cordially. 'One of the best.'

'I borrowed it to read in the train. Now will you kindly tell me what you are doing in my room, Mr Mulliner?'

Cyril smote his forehead.

'Of course. I remember now. It all comes back to me. She told me you had taken it. And, what's more, I've suddenly recollected something which clears you completely. I was hustled and bustled at the end of the journey. I sprang to my feet, hurled bags on to the platform – in a word, lost my head. And, like a chump, I went and left my copy of "Strychnine in the Soup" in the train. Well, I can only apologize.'

'You can not only apologize. You can also tell me what you are doing in my room?'

'What I am doing in your room?'

'Exactly.'

'Ah!' said Cyril, sitting down on the bed. 'You may well ask.'

'I *have* asked. Three times.'

Cyril closed his eyes. For some reason, his mind seemed cloudy and not at its best.

'If you are proposing to go to sleep here, Mr Mulliner,' said Lady Bassett, 'tell me, and I shall know what to do about it.'

The phrase touched a chord in Cyril's memory. He recollected now his reasons for being where he was. Opening his eyes, he fixed them on her.

'Lady Bassett,' he said, 'you are, I believe, an explorer?'

'I am.'

'In the course of your explorations, you have wandered through many a jungle in many a distant land?'

'I have.'

'Tell me, Lady Bassett,' said Cyril keenly, 'while making a pest of yourself to the denizens of those jungles, did you notice one thing? I allude to the fact that Love is everywhere – aye, even in the jungle. Love, independent of bounds and frontiers, of nationality and species, works its spell on every living thing. So that, no matter whether an individual be a Congo native, an American song-writer, a jaguar, an armadillo, a bespoke tailor, or a tsetse-tsetse fly, he will infallibly seek his mate. So why shouldn't an interior decorator and designer of ornamental gardens? I put this to you, Lady Bassett.'

'Mr Mulliner,' said his room-mate, 'you are blotto!'

Cyril waved his hand in a spacious gesture, and fell off the bed.

'Blotto I may be,' he said, resuming his seat, 'but, none the less, argue as you will, you can't get away from the fact that I love your daughter Amelia.'

There was a tense pause.

'What did you say?' cried Lady Bassett.

'When?' said Cyril absently, for he had fallen into a daydream and, as far as the intervening blankets would permit, was playing 'This little pig went to market' with his companion's toes.

'Did I hear you say . . . my daughter Amelia?'

'Grey-eyed girl, medium height, sort of browny-red hair,' said Cyril, to assist her memory. 'Dash it, you *must* know Amelia. She goes everywhere. And let me tell you something, Mrs – I've forgotten your name. We're going to be married, if I can obtain her foul mother's consent. Speaking as an old friend, what would you say the chances were?'

'Extremely slight.'

'Eh?'

'Seeing that I *am* Amelia's mother . . . '

Cyril blinked, genuinely surprised.

'Why, so you are! I didn't recognize you. Have you been there all the time?'

'I have.'

Suddenly Cyril's gaze hardened. He drew himself up stiffly.

'What are you doing in my bed?' he demanded.

'This is not your bed.'

'Then whose is it?'

'Mine.'

Cyril shrugged his shoulders helplessly.

'Well, it all looks very funny to me,' he said. 'I suppose I must believe your story, but, I repeat, I consider the whole thing odd, and I propose to institute very strict enquiries. I may tell you that I happen to know the ringleaders. I wish you a very hearty good night.'

*

It was perhaps an hour later that Cyril, who had been walking on the terrace in deep thought, repaired once more to the Blue Room in quest of information. Running over the details of the recent interview in his head, he had suddenly discovered that there was a point which had not been satisfactorily cleared up.

'I say,' he said.

Lady Bassett looked up from her book, plainly annoyed.

'Have you no bedroom of your own, Mr Mulliner?'

'Oh, yes,' said Cyril. 'They've bedded me out in the Moat Room. But there was something I wanted you to tell me.'

'Well?'

'Did you say I might or mightn't?'

'Might or mightn't what?'

'Marry Amelia?'

'No. You may not.'

'No?'

'No!'

'Oh!' said Cyril. 'Well, pip-pip once more.'

It was a moody Cyril Mulliner who withdrew to the Moat Room. He now realized the position of affairs. The mother of the girl he loved refused to accept him as an eligible suitor. A dickens of a situation to be in, felt Cyril, sombrely unshoeing himself.

Then he brightened a little. His life, he reflected,

might be wrecked, but he still had two-thirds of 'Strychnine in the Soup' to read.

At the moment when the train reached Barkley Regis station, Cyril had just got to the bit where Detective Inspector Mould looks through the half-open cellar door and, drawing in his breath with a sharp, hissing sound, recoils in horror. It was obviously going to be good. He was just about to proceed to the dressing-table where, he presumed, the footman had placed the book on unpacking his bag, when an icy stream seemed to flow down the centre of his spine and the room and its contents danced before him.

Once more he had remembered that he had left the volume in the train.

He uttered an animal cry and tottered to a chair.

The subject of bereavement is one that has often been treated powerfully by poets, who have run the whole gamut of the emotions while laying bare for us the agony of those who have lost parents, wives, children, gazelles, money, fame, dogs, cats, doves, sweethearts, horses, and even collar-studs. But no poet has yet treated of the most poignant bereavement of all – that of the man half-way through a detective story who finds himself at bedtime without the book.

Cyril did not care to think of the night that lay before him. Already his brain was lashing itself from side to side like a wounded snake as it sought for some explanation of Inspector Mould's strange behaviour.

Horatio Slingsby was an author who could be relied on to keep faith with his public. He was not the sort of man to fob the reader off in the next chapter with the statement that what had made Inspector Mould look horrified was the fact that he had suddenly remembered that he had forgotten all about the letter his wife had given him to post. If looking through cellar doors disturbed a Slingsby detective, it was because a dismembered corpse lay there, or at least a severed hand.

A soft moan, as of some thing in torment, escaped Cyril. What to do? What to do? Even a makeshift substitute for 'Strychnine in the Soup' was beyond his reach. He knew so well what he would find if he went to the library in search of something to read. Sir Mortimer Wingham was heavy and country-squire-ish. His wife affected strange religions. Their literature was in keeping with their tastes. In the library there would be books on Ba-ha-ism, volumes in old leather of the Rural Encyclopædia, 'My Two Years in Sunny Ceylon', by the Rev. Orlo Waterbury . . . but of anything that would interest Scotland Yard, of anything with a bit of blood in it and a corpse or two into which a fellow could get his teeth, not a trace.

What, then, coming right back to it, to do?

And suddenly, as if in answer to the question, came the solution. Electrified, he saw the way out.

The hour was now well advanced. By this time Lady Bassett must surely be asleep. 'Strychnine in the Soup' would be lying on the table beside her bed. All he had to do was to creep in and grab it.

The more he considered the idea, the better it looked. It was not as if he did not know the way to Lady Bassett's room or the topography of it when he got there. It seemed to him as if most of his later life had been spent in Lady Bassett's room. He could find his way about it with his eyes shut.

He hesitated no longer. Donning a dressing-gown, he left his room and hurried along the passage.

Pushing open the door of the Blue Room and closing it softly behind him, Cyril stood for a moment full of all those emotions which come to man revisiting some long-familiar spot. There the dear old room was, just the same as ever. How it all came back to him! The place was in darkness, but that did not deter him. He knew where the bed-table was, and he made for it with stealthy steps.

In the manner in which Cyril Mulliner advanced towards the bed-table there was much which would have reminded Lady Bassett, had she been an eye-witness, of the furtive prowl of the Lesser Iguanodon tracking its prey. In only one respect did Cyril and this creature of the wild differ in their technique. Iguanodons – and this applies not only to the Lesser but to the Larger Iguanodon – seldom, if ever, trip over cords on the floor and bring the lamps to which they are attached crashing to the ground like a ton of bricks.

Cyril did. Scarcely had he snatched up the book and placed it in the pocket of his dressing-gown, when his foot became entangled in the trailing cord and the lamp on the table leaped nimbly into the air and, to the accompaniment of a sound not unlike that made by a hundred plates coming apart simultaneously in the hands of a hundred scullery-maids, nosedived to the floor and became a total loss.

At the same moment, Lady Bassett, who had been chasing a bat out of the window, stepped in from the balcony and switched on the lights.

To say that Cyril Mulliner was taken aback would be to understate the facts. Nothing like his recent misadventure had happened to him since his eleventh year, when, going surreptitiously to his mother's cupboard for jam, he had jerked three shelves down on his head, containing milk, butter, home-made preserves, pickles, cheese, eggs, cakes, and potted-meat. His feelings on the present occasion closely paralleled that boyhood thrill.

Lady Bassett also appeared somewhat discomposed.

'You!' she said.

Cyril nodded, endeavouring the while to smile in a reassuring manner.

'Hullo!' he said.

His hostess's manner was now one of unmistakable displeasure.

'Am I not to have a moment of privacy, Mr Mulliner?' she asked severely. 'I am, I trust, a broad-minded woman, but I cannot approve of this idea of communal bedrooms.'

Cyril made an effort to be conciliatory.

'I do keep coming in, don't I?' he said.

'You do,' agreed Lady Bassett. 'Sir Mortimer informed me, on learning that I had been given this room, that it was supposed to be haunted. Had I known that it was haunted by you, Mr Mulliner, I should have packed up and gone to the local inn.'

Cyril bowed his head. The censure, he could not but feel, was deserved.

'I admit,' he said, 'that my conduct has been open to criticism. In extenuation, I can but plead my great love. This is no idle social call, Lady Bassett. I looked in because I wished to take up again this matter of my marrying your daughter Amelia. You say I can't. Why can't I? Answer me that, Lady Bassett.'

'I have other views for Amelia,' said Lady Bassett stiffly. 'When my daughter gets married it will not be to a spineless, invertebrate product of our modern hot-house civilization, but to a strong, upstanding, keen-eyed, two-fisted he-man of the open spaces. I have no wish to hurt your feelings, Mr Mulliner,' she continued, more kindly, 'but you must admit that you are, when all is said and done, a pipsqueak.'

'I deny it,' cried Cyril warmly. 'I don't even know what a pipsqueak is.'

'A pipsqueak is a man who has never seen the sun rise beyond the reaches of the Lower Zambezi; who would not know what to do if faced by a charging rhinoceros. What, pray, would you do if faced by a charging rhinoceros, Mr Mulliner?'

'I am not likely,' said Cyril, 'to move in the same social circles as charging rhinoceri.'

'Or take another simple case, such as happens every day. Suppose you are crossing a rude bridge over a stream in Equatorial Africa. You have been thinking of a hundred trifles and are in a reverie. From this you wake to discover that in the branches overhead a python is extending its fangs towards you. At the same time, you observe that at one end of the bridge is a crouching puma; at the other are two head hunters – call them Pat and Mike – with poisoned blow-pipes to their lips. Below, half hidden in the stream, is an alligator. What would you do in such a case, Mr Mulliner?'

Cyril weighed the point.

'I should feel embarrassed,' he had to admit. 'I shouldn't know where to look.'

Lady Bassett laughed an amused, scornful little laugh.

'Precisely. Such a situation would not, however, disturb Lester Mapledurham.'

'Lester Mapledurham!'

'The man who is to marry my daughter Amelia. He asked me for her hand shortly after dinner.'

Cyril reeled. The blow, falling so suddenly and unexpectedly, had made him feel boneless. And yet, he felt, he might have expected this. These explorers and big-game hunters stick together.

'In a situation such as I have outlined, Lester Mapledurham would simply drop from the bridge, wait till the alligator made its rush, insert a stout stick between its jaws, and then hit it in the eye with a spear, being careful to avoid its lashing tail. He would then drift down-stream and land at some safer spot. That is the type of man I wish for as a son-in-law.'

Cyril left the room without a word. Not even the fact that he now had 'Strychnine in the Soup' in his possession could cheer his mood of unrelieved blackness. Back in his room, he tossed the book moodily on to the bed and began to pace the floor. And he had scarcely completed two laps when the door opened.

For an instant, when he heard the click of the latch, Cyril supposed that his visitor must be Lady Bassett, who, having put two and two together on discovering her loss, had come to demand her property back. And he cursed the rashness which had led him to fling it so carelessly upon the bed, in full view.

But it was not Lady Bassett. The intruder was Lester Mapledurham. Clad in a suit of pyjamas which in their general colour scheme reminded Cyril of a boudoir he had recently decorated for a Society poetess, he stood with folded arms, his keen eyes fixed menacingly on the young man.

'Give me those jewels!' said Lester Mapledurham.

Cyril was at a loss.

'Jewels?'

'Jewels!'

'What jewels?'

Lester Mapledurham tossed his head impatiently.

'I don't know what jewels. They may be the Wingham Pearls or the Bassett Diamonds or the Simpson Sapphires. I'm not sure which room it was I saw you coming out of.'

Cyril began to understand.

'Oh, did you see me coming out of a room?'

'I did. I heard a crash and, when I looked out, you were hurrying along the corridor.'

'I can explain everything,' said Cyril. 'I had just been having a chat with Lady Bassett on a personal matter. Nothing to do with diamonds.'

'You're sure?' said Mapledurham.

'Oh, rather,' said Cyril. 'We talked about rhinoceri and pythons and her daughter Amelia and alligators and all that sort of thing, and then I came away.'

Lester Mapledurham seemed only half convinced.

'H'm!' he said. 'Well, if anything is missing in the morning, I shall know what to do about it.' His eye fell on the bed. 'Hullo!' he went on, with sudden animation. 'Slingsby's latest? Well, well! I've been wanting to get hold of this. I hear it's good. The *Leeds Mercury* says: "These gripping pages . . . ".'

He turned to the door, and with a hideous pang of agony Cyril perceived that it was plainly his intention to take the book with him. It was swinging lightly from a bronzed hand about the size of a medium ham.

'Here!' he cried, vehemently.

Lester Mapledurham turned.

'Well?'

'Oh, nothing,' said Cyril. 'Just good night.'

He flung himself face downwards on the bed as the door closed, cursing himself for the craven cowardice which had kept him from snatching the book from the explorer. There had been a moment when he had almost nerved himself to the deed, but it was followed by another moment in which he had caught the other's eye. And it was as if he had found himself exchanging glances with Lady Bassett's charging rhinoceros.

And now, thanks to this pusillanimity, he was once more 'Strychnine in the Soup'-less.

How long Cyril lay there, a prey to the gloomiest thoughts, he could not have said. He was aroused from his meditations by the sound of the door opening again.

Lady Bassett stood before him. It was plain that she was deeply moved. In addition to resembling Wallace Beery and Victor McLaglen, she now had a distinct look of George Bancroft.

She pointed a quivering finger at Cyril.

'You hound!' she cried. 'Give me that book!'

Cyril maintained his poise with a strong effort.

'What book?'

'The book you sneaked out of my room?'

'Has someone sneaked a book out of your room?' Cyril struck his forehead. 'Great heavens!' he cried.

'Mr Mulliner,' said Lady Bassett coldly, 'more book and less gibbering!'

Cyril raised a hand.

'I know who's got your book. Lester Mapledurham!'

'Don't be absurd.'

'He has, I tell you. As I was on my way to your room just now, I saw him coming out, carrying something in a furtive manner. I remember wondering a bit at the time. He's in the Clock Room. If we pop along there now, we shall just catch him red-handed.'

Lady Bassett reflected.

'It is impossible,' she said at length. 'He is incapable of such an act. Lester Mapledurham is a man who once killed a lion with a sardine-opener.'

'The very worst sort,' said Cyril. 'Ask anyone.'

'And he is engaged to my daughter.' Lady Bassett paused. 'Well, he won't be long, if I find that what you say is true. Come, Mr Mulliner!'

Together the two passed down the silent passage. At the door of the Clock Room they paused. A light streamed from beneath it. Cyril pointed silently to this sinister evidence of reading in bed, and noted that his companion stiffened and said something to herself in an undertone in what appeared to be some sort of native dialect.

The next moment she had flung the door open and, with a spring like that of a crouching zebu, had leaped to the bed and wrenched the book from Lester Mapledurham's hands.

'So!' said Lady Bassett.

'So!' said Cyril, feeling that he could not do better than follow the lead of such a woman.

'Hullo!' said Lester Mapledurham, surprised. 'Something the matter?'

'So it was you who stole my book!'

'Your book?' said Lester Mapledurham. 'I borrowed this from Mr Mulliner there.'

'A likely story!' said Cyril. 'Lady Bassett is aware that I left my copy of "Strychnine in the Soup" in the train.'

'Certainly,' said Lady Bassett. 'It's no use talking, young man, I have caught you with the goods. And let me tell you one thing that may be of interest. If you think that, after a dastardly act like this, you are going to marry Amelia, forget it!'

'Wipe it right out of your mind,' said Cyril.

'But listen—!'

'I will not listen. Come, Mr Mulliner.'

She left the room, followed by Cyril. For some moments they walked in silence.

'A merciful escape,' said Cyril

'For whom?'

'For Amelia. My gosh, think of her tied to a man like that. Must be a relief to you to feel that she's going to marry a respectable interior decorator.'

Lady Bassett halted. They were standing outside the Moat Room now. She looked at Cyril, her eyebrows raised.

'Are you under the impression, Mr Mulliner,' she said, 'that, on the strength of what has happened, I intend to accept you as a son-in-law?'

Cyril reeled.

'Don't you?'

'Certainly not.'

Something inside Cyril seemed to snap. Recklessness descended upon him. He became for a space a thing of courage and fire, like the African leopard in the mating season.

'Oh!' he said.

And, deftly whisking 'Strychnine in the Soup' from his companion's hand, he darted into his room, banged the door, and bolted it.

'Mr Mulliner!'

It was Lady Bassett's voice, coming pleadingly through the woodwork. It was plain that she was shaken to the core, and Cyril smiled sardonically. He was in a position to dictate terms.

'Give me that book, Mr Mulliner!'

'Certainly not,' said Cyril. 'I intend to read it myself. I hear good reports of it on every side. The *Peebles Intelligencer* says: "Vigorous and absorbing".'

A low wail from the other side of the door answered him.

'Of course,' said Cyril, suggestively, 'if it were my future mother-in-law who was speaking, her word would naturally be law.'

There was a silence outside.

'Very well,' said Lady Bassett.

'I may marry Amelia?'

'You may.'

Cyril unbolted the door.

'Come – Mother,' he said, in a soft, kindly voice. 'We will read it together, down in the library.'

Lady Bassett was still shaken.

'I hope I have acted for the best,' she said.

'You have,' said Cyril.

'You will make Amelia a good husband?'

'Grade A,' Cyril assured her.

'Well, even if you don't,' said Lady Bassett resignedly, 'I can't go to bed without that book. I had just got to the bit where Inspector Mould is trapped in the underground den of the Faceless Fiend.'

Cyril quivered.

'*Is* there a Faceless Fiend?' he cried.

'There are two Faceless Fiends,' said Lady Bassett.

'My gosh!' said Cyril. 'Let's hurry.'

Pelham Grenville Wodehouse (always known as 'Plum') wrote more than ninety novels and some three hundred short stories over 73 years. He is widely recognised as the greatest 20th-century writer of humour in the English language.

Perhaps best known for the escapades of Bertie Wooster and Jeeves, Wodehouse also created the world of Blandings Castle, home to Lord Emsworth and his cherished pig, the Empress of Blandings. His stories include gems concerning the irrepressible and disreputable Ukridge; Psmith, the elegant socialist; the ever-so-slightly-unscrupulous Fifth Earl of Ickenham, better known as Uncle Fred; and those related by Mr Mulliner, the charming raconteur of The Angler's Rest, and the Oldest Member at the Golf Club.

In 1936 he was awarded the Mark Twain Prize for 'having made an outstanding and lasting contribution to the happiness of the world'. He was made a Doctor of Letters by Oxford University in 1939 and in 1975, aged 93, he was knighted by Queen Elizabeth II. He died shortly afterwards, on St Valentine's Day.

ALSO AVAILABLE IN THIS SERIES

Featuring

The Amazing Hat Mystery

Uncle Fred Flits By

Trouble Down at Tudsleigh

Featuring

Goodbye to All Cats

Ukridge's Dog College

Ukridge's Accident Syndicate

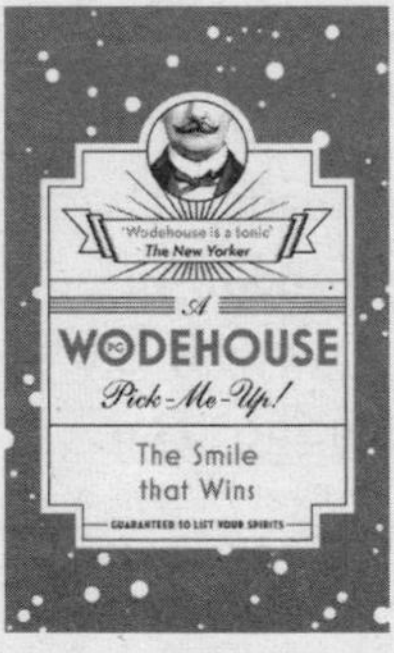

Featuring

The Smile that Wins

Jeeves and the Song of Songs

The Great Sermon Handicap